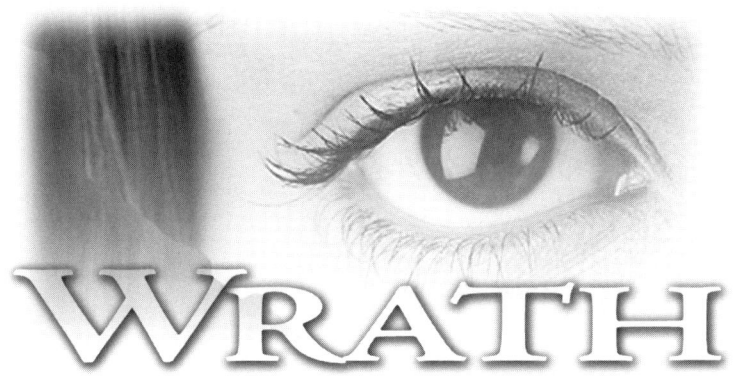

Claire Hollis, Ph.D.

Claire Hollis, Ph.D.

WRATH

ISBN 0-9673122-5-6

Library of Congress Control Number: 2005901402

Copyright© 2005 by Claire Hollis

Printed in the United States of America

Published by Warfare Publications
3457 W. Kenyon Ave.
Tampa, FL 33614 USA
(813) 935-4673
Fax: (813) 908-0228
E-mail: WarfareP@aol.com
Web site: www.warfareplus.com

All rights reserved under International Copyright Law. No part of this publication may be reproduced, stored in a retrieval system, or transmitted, in whole or in part, in any form or by any means, electronic, mechanical, photocopying, recording, or otherwise, without the prior express consent of the publisher. Unless otherwise indicated, all scripture references are from the authorized King James Version of the Bible.

Wrath is the fourth book of a series.

Wrath

Claire Hollis, Ph.D.

A Note From The Author

This book is prophetic in nature. It is a fictitious account of what could happen soon on planet earth based on Bible prophecy. *WRATH* is the final book in a series of four, *and* continues a chain of events that climax the end of time as we know it. JJ and Lynn have been entertaining two house guests who unleash supernatural powers that far exceed that of Bishop John and President Catlin.

The story begins with the first book in the series, *THE LIGHT*. JJ and Lynn Murphy visit their nephew in the mysterious small town of Centerville. They uncover demonic secrets that have remained hidden for years. Rulers of the dark world retaliate by issuing a death contract against them.

The second book, *DELAYED INVASION* continues with JJ and Lynn traveling to Washington, D.C. to get a book published. While there, they discover that a U.S. military crew stationed in Germany mysteriously intercepts a plot to overthrow the governments of the world by disguising themselves as beings from outer space. JJ and Lynn witness a kidnapping which puts them in the middle of this top-secret invasion plan.

The same characters in the previous two books find themselves in life threatening situations in the third book of the series *DECEIVED*. President Catlin and Bishop John have been successful at deceiving most of the world by pretending to be holy and religious, and performing miracles. Now, JJ and Lynn have to make the decision to either obey President Catlin by receiving the computer chip on their forehead or hand, or to die.

I recommend that you read all of the books to really get to know and appreciate the main characters, and to receive the full impact of the series.

Claire Hollis, Ph.D.

Claire Hollis, Ph.D.

WRATH

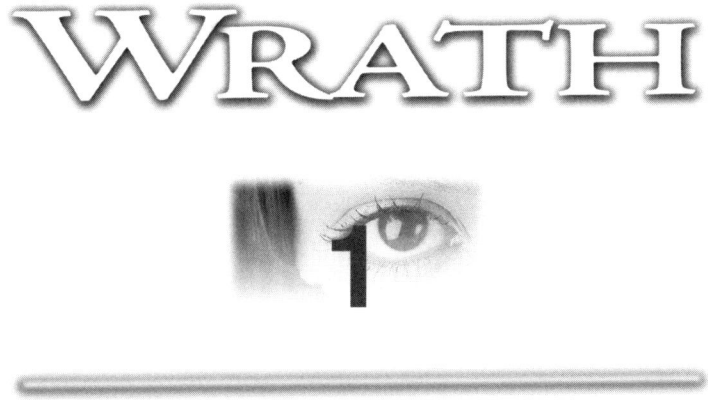

1

J and Lynn Murphy along with their eight children and their families lay in a heap on the floor where President Catlin, in a fit of rage, grabbed the guard's gun and just started shooting. Blood was everywhere. It was a horrible sight to behold. For that reason President Catlin had ordered this bloody scene to televised world wide. He wanted to send a message to the world; a warning that this would happen to anyone who refused to accept the mark that he had established which enabled them to buy or sell.

Little did Catlin realize that he would not have been able to touch the Murphy family if God Almighty had not allowed it. Neither did President Catlin nor any of his military guards see the mighty angels who appeared at this deadly scene and quickly ushered all of them into the presence of God. Death had no sting for the Murphy family. They were all happy, excited, joyful and rejoicing as their souls were being escorted away by the angels.

WRATH 2

Everyone on the planet was required to give a DNA sample to the world government for identification purposes. This sample was put into the World Computer Bank. In this manner the government had information on every living person. Catlin and Bishop John instituted that a computer chip be implanted in everyone's hand or head. The chip was so minute that it could not be seen with the naked eye and was implanted painlessly. A law was passed that no one could buy or sell without the chip, and anyone who was caught helping someone who did not have a chip was executed. Everyone's chip contained the numbers "666." All Christians were registered in the computer bank, but not a single one had received the chip!

One government controlled the earth. The dominating powers of this ruling system were two young men, President Catlin and Bishop John. Satan himself had entered into the body of President Catlin. Satan had done so in the exact same manner that he had entered into the body of Judas Iscariot over two thousand years ago when he betrayed Jesus Christ.

Lana was second in command in the hierarchy of Satan's demonic kingdom. President Catlin (satan) granted her the privilege of possessing the body of Bishop John. Then he appointed Bishop John to become the leader of the world religious system called Unity.

Even though Satan and Lana were spirit beings, they have taken control and completely possessed the bodies of President Catlin and Bishop John. Spirit beings must have a human body to work out of, and these bodies were perfect! Together they ruled the earth, with one in charge of the government and the other in charge of religion.

Now the pair was always seen together. Both men were in their early thirties and extremely handsome. Bishop John stood about six foot tall and reeked of purity. His sandy blonde hair flowed to his shoulders. His big blue eyes captivated the souls of everyone, and when he spoke, it was as though honey dripped from his lips. He was so smooth-talking, full of charm and charisma that he was able to deceive most everyone. Although, there was a small minority of *religious* people that he had been unable to deceive. This is the group that had been connected with the Murphy family. The ones that President Catlin killed.

President Catlin's appearance was quite a contrast to that of Bishop John. He had beautiful olive skin, dark eyes that could penetrate right through you. He recently had his hair cut short and had started a trend in men's hair fashion because everyone wanted to look like him. His square jaw line added to his manly appearance along with the dark shadow that appeared if he didn't shave twice a day.

Together, Bishop John and President Catlin were stunning sights to behold. Their striking features gained them instant attention and admiration. Both men were approximately the same height, and were so handsome that they would stand out in any crowd. They were perfect shells for Satan and Lana to operate through. If only the people of the world could have seen past these gorgeous exteriors to the hideous monsters that lurked underneath.

President Catlin and Bishop John are soaking in the worship and power that is being bestowed on them. Satan is now in his full glory being the ruler of the world. Bishop John has ordered that a statue of President Catlin be erected in the new Jewish Temple in Jerusalem and has required everyone who entered to bow down and worship the statue or be put to death. In every nation, at exactly three o'clock in the afternoon everyone was forced to bow to the ground in worship of President Catlin. Together they have deceived the people of the world into believing that they were doing a good and godly act to destroy anyone that was not loyal to President Catlin, the world government, and the world religious system.

Catlin has been controlling the planet now for several years. Things have been going smoothly and there is world wide peace. Everyone belongs to the Unity Church and they worship King Catlin. Everyone, this is, except for the small group of renegades who call themselves Christians. They refused to worship President Catlin.

Claire Hollis, Ph.D.

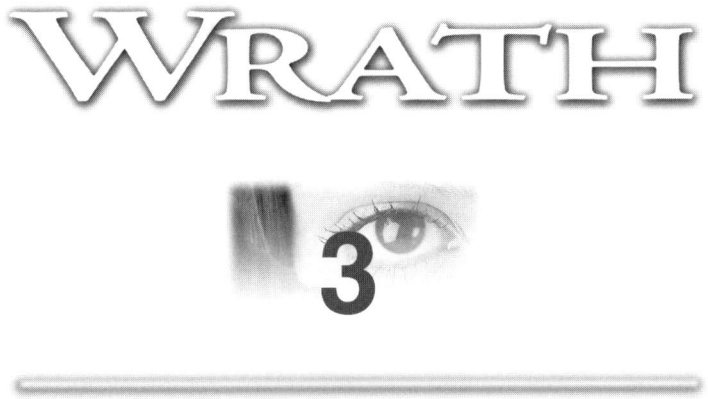

WRATH
3

The entire Murphy family had been the first ones to be slaughtered as a warning to the remnant groups that still refused to accept the computer chip. President Catlin had made the registration of every human on the planet mandatory, but as far as the mark with the computer chip, he had allowed each individual to decide for themselves if they would receive the chip or not. He could track down any person on the planet who had a chip. They could decide to accept the computer chip to be implanted into their body, or they could refuse it and die. To avoid death the remnant group had all gone into hiding.

President Catlin and Bishop John called a meeting of all the top world officials with very little effort. It was as if the delegates were under some kind of hypnotic spell, wanting to do anything to please Catlin and Bishop John. Their minds were fixed on pleasing and worshiping the two that were leading the world.

The officials were in their assigned places awaiting the arrival of their leaders, when suddenly the door swung open and the two emerged in more splendor than any had yet to see. President Catlin and Bishop John glided into the room wearing long robes with dazzling crowns on their heads. President Catlin's crown was bigger than Bishop John's, and glistened with large sparkling gems. The jewels that adorned both their garments were more spectacular than anyone had ever seen at one time. The beauty of the robes was so dazzling and breathtaking that it was almost blinding. President Catlin's robe was purple and he radiated majesty and pride. Bishop John's crown was made of pure gold and his robe was white to symbolize purity. Across his chest embroidered with gold thread was the word "*UNITY*".

Immediately upon the entrance of the two men, the officials fell down with their faces to the floor in reverence. Satan (President Catlin) allowed them to stay prostrate for several minutes while he gloried in the worship. How he loved to be worshiped....it empowered him! Finally, he released them to take their seats so that the meeting could get underway.

Bishop John addressed the group. "We have a slight problem on our hands, and I need everyone in this room to help me to resolve it." He walked slowly around the room eyeing each individual closely. "You all remember JJ and Lynn Murphy that you saw laying dead on television, as a warning to all those who refuse to honor and worship President Catlin." The officials all nodded to one another in agreement as Catlin and Bishop John exchanged haughty glances. "Well, it seems that there are those who want to follow in their footsteps. We all have to work together and find them and kill them. You all know that one rotten apple can spoil the whole group. Well, if we don't get rid of all these bad apples they may try to overthrow your governments. We all need to work together with a plan to rid ourselves of the last thing that is keeping this world from being a perfect paradise.

President Catlin had seated himself with superiority at the head of the long black table. His seat looked more like a throne and was elevated above the rest. Bishop John continued to slowly glide around the men as he continued his oration.

"The threat of death is not working. They're not afraid to die. All these renegade Christian groups consider themselves dead to their own desires already and they are on a suicide mission to overthrow our government and our church. They have been communicating with each other world wide through the internet. They have a secret code in the computer that we are not able to break. A mysterious block prevents us from deciphering their codes. We were able to de-code it to a certain point and then it's like we hit a blank wall." Lana, who was inhabiting the body of Bishop John, knew exactly what the block was. It had been supernaturally put there by a power much bigger than President Catlin. Bishop John just kept on talking for fear that Satan (President Catlin) might be reading his mind. "This little remnant group could cause problems if we don't stamp them out!"

The leader of the Arabic nations raised his hand to ask a question. Bishop John nodded to him and he stood up. "I have been wondering how these people survive without being able to buy and sell?"

President Catlin had been silent until now, but as he heard this question being asked his eyes began to glow with a reddish hue and a grotesque snarl crossed his face. He lunged forward as he stood, pointing his finger in everyone's face. "All these who refuse to follow the only true church that we have established began to store up food and supplies before the new millennium. They expected that there would be all kinds of Y2K problems, with computer shut downs, they envisioned planes falling out of the sky, banks closing, lack of food supplies, electrical shortages, etc. For this reason they all began to store up and prepare to sustain themselves. In answer to your question they are prepared to exist for who knows how long. They are all registered, so we know WHO they are, but we are unable to locate them because they don't have a computer chip. As you know we can locate anyone on this planet in a moment's notice if they have a chip, but these renegade groups stay on the go all the time. Whenever we get close to one of their little groups they mysteriously disappear. It is as if someone informs them of our plans." President Catlin knew all too well that it was God's Angels who were directing the small groups, but he wasn't about to tell anyone.

"They have a leader! JJ and Lynn Murphy have a nephew who lived in a town called Centerville in the United States. Whenever we rid ourselves of the Murphy family, everyone who belonged to this rebellious group began to look to JJ's nephew, Pastor Terry, for direction. Although he was a small town preacher, he also had more computer knowledge than anyone on this planet. He's the one who developed that communication system that we're unable to penetrate.

"There are two other people that this group looks to for direction. Before we were able to rid ourselves of the Murphy's, they had two men who came to stay at their home as house guests. They are two weird looking characters. They look like two sacks of potatoes." A slight chuckle filled the room from the group who was sitting with their interpreter head phones. "Their clothing is made of a burlap type material. They wear the same thing every day. They were wearing these clothes even before we did away with the Murphy's. One of the men calls himself Eli and the other calls himself Mo. These two disappeared from the Murphy's house right after the slaughter, and we haven't been able to find them since, but we do know that they all keep in touch with each other via the internet."

Satan suspected that these two men were the end-time witnesses described in the Bible, but would never reveal this information. Lana wondered also, but was too afraid to even bring up the conversation.

President Catlin placed both hands palms down, on the table and leaned forward. "I want a plan devised to get rid of all these people, but I especially want Terry and Bobbi Murphy and their son, Joshua, killed along with these two visitors that were living with the Murphy's. We can't have true peace and unity on this planet until we rid ourselves of these undesirables. Does anyone have any ideas?" President Catlin eyed each man individually with a sharp look.

The leader of the oriental nations was wearing a beautiful silk robe of many colors. He raised his hand and when Catlin acknowledged him, he bowed before him, and then bowed to the rest of the men at the table. "Why don't we devise a plan to get them all at one place at the same time? Then the rest will be easy. As long as they are scattered all over the earth, it could take us years to flush them all out."

"Excellent." President Catlin paused for a moment, and then repeated, "Excellent! We could offer them asylum. We can say that we have changed our minds and decided to let their little group live in peace, and even offer them a country to live in and pledge to them that they will be left alone to worship any way they choose. We can offer them transportation to that country and provide all the necessary provisions for them to become a free nation, and they will not be expected to have a computer chip. When we round up every last one of them, then—BOOM!" President Catlin slammed his fist onto the table, "We'll annihilate them off the face of the earth! Great suggestion!"

It was Satan's demonic power over the leader of the oriental nation that caused him to respond with this idea, but Catlin wanted the rest of the group to feel as if they had a part in the world decisions. He was such an expert at deceiving humans, and it enraged him not to be able to deceive the Christians. President Catlin's evil eyes met with Bishop John's, and with an extremely positive voice, he cries out, "EXCELLENT SUGGESTION!"

Bishop John responded to the idea by saying, "I'll hold a world TV press conference immediately with the Unity Television Network (UTN), and have it aired every few minutes on the internet and television. This word will go out all over the world. We'll be free of this rebellion and then nothing can interfere with our peace and unity."

Bishop John asked everyone to stand while he prayed. "We give all honor and glory and reverence to our leader King Catlin." What was it that Lana had just said? Those weren't her words, Bishop John had never referred to President Catlin as King Catlin before, where had they come from? The prayer continued, "We worship you King Catlin as the King of Kings and Lord of Lords" "There it is again," Lana thought to herself as she spoke out with Bishop John's manly voice. She concluded with, "Amen." When she looked around, all were prostrate on the floor paying homage to their leader.

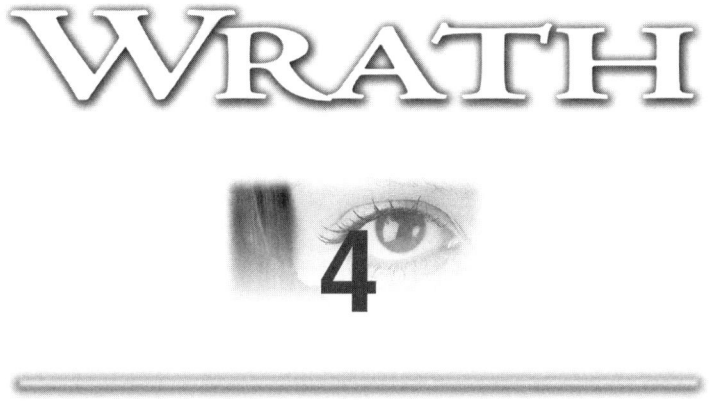

WRATH 4

The next morning, newscasters, cameras, and microphones surrounded Catlin as he stepped up to the podium for the worldwide press conference. The media filled the room. Bishop John introduced Catlin to the UTN audience as "King" Catlin and from that moment forth he was never referred to as president again. He was known as King of the Universe.

King Catlin stepped up to the microphones and smiled very lovingly to all the world. His eyes sparkled with charm. He was so charming and handsome it was easy for him to captivate the world's population. Everyone honored and adored him because he had brought peace to a world that had been filled with war and chaos. His purple robe and dazzling crown were so breathtaking that they alone demanded respect.

"I have been consulting with Bishop John about all those who have chosen not to become a part of our world government. At first our decision was to destroy all those who opposed the peace and unity that I have brought upon the earth. Now it has been decided by the world government to let you live. We want you to live in peace and allow you to worship your God in freedom and without fear. Because we all believe in *Unity*, we have agreed to let you all unite in one place and dwell together. I have instructed every airport to give you priority placement, and give you access to the first flights available, at no cost to you. I am commanding anyone that you come in contact with to give you transportation to the nearest airport, where you will be taken to the land of Israel where you can all unite safely together. We are evacuating an area in order to make room for you. This information will be broadcast on TV, radio, shortwave, newspapers, computers and even by public PA systems so that everyone will be made aware to help you. You can be assured that you are not to be harmed. I have made it a law that anyone who harms you will be put to death."

The people listening were quite puzzled at the King's remarks, but no one dared make a comment for fear of him.

After making the appeal to all his enemies who were in hiding, he left the television cameras and he and Bishop John went directly to Jerusalem. It was the King's idea not to travel the conventional way. He and Lana went the demonic route and simply translated themselves, so they could be there in seconds. He wanted to be worshiped and the only place that seemed to give him satisfaction was the temple in Jerusalem. Catlin had made a truce with Israel and had built them a temple near the site of the former Dome of the Rock. When the meteorite destroyed the Dome and unearthed the Ark of the Covenant, he had allowed it to be put into the special room of the new temple that was called the Holy of Holies, but in a fit of anger on the same day that he killed all the Murphy family, he went into the Holy of Holies and knocked over the Ark of the Covenant and spit on it. He then requested that Bishop John erect a large golden statue of himself to stand where the Ark had been.

When satan, (in the body of King Catlin) would go into this holy room, he would become empowered. He reveled in the worship of man, but this special place of worship was like an addiction to him. He couldn't seem to stay away from it. He was drawn to it to the point that he was taking chances going there by translating himself instead of taking a jet. It was becoming a daily habit. He would always come away with a crazed look in his eyes. His extremely good looking appearance was beginning to change. His facial features were beginning to show what evil lurked inside. He had recently developed a hideous laugh and a nervous habit of taking his fingertips and rubbing them over the precious stones in his crown. The stones in his crown were absolutely brilliant. It almost looked like laser beams were shooting out from them.

Claire Hollis, Ph.D.

WRATH

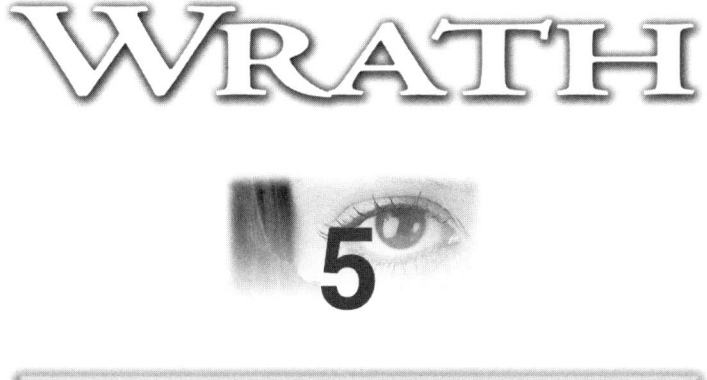

Most believers in Jesus Christ had already been martyred. Those that weren't killed by the sword had seen death by hunger and wild beast. There was only a small remnant left and after hearing the news, they all immediately logged onto the internet with their secret code and began corresponding with each other.

Terry and Bobbi Murphy were a small town preacher and wife until his uncle JJ and aunt Lynn came along and changed their lives forever. The entire Christian world began to look to them for direction after the death of his uncle JJ. They weren't sophisticated like most leaders. Terry bore a strong resemblance to his father with his olive complexion, black hair and tall frame. Bobbi was so cute with her sparkling big blue eyes, freckles on her nose, and beautiful thick red hair. They were certainly a good looking couple. The home they lived in and the clothes they wore were very modest, but in excellent taste.

Pastor Terry, his wife Bobbi and Eli and Mo were now put into the position of making the decision for the entire group. Everyone trusted these four as their leaders and were eager to follow whatever they advised them to do.

It was obvious to Pastor Terry and Bobbi that Mo and Eli were very special people, and that they had been in the presence of God. They had spent hours just soaking up all the spiritual revelation that these two were imparting to them.

Together as they were discussing the newscast, Pastor Terry just couldn't hold in all his questions about these two any longer. He looked straight into Mo and Eli's eyes, and asked them boldly, "I have to ask you this question! Are you really Moses and Elijah?"

Mo and Eli looked at each other as Pastor Terry continued, "Many Bible scholars believe that it will be Moses and Elijah that will return to earth during the last days. Bobbi and I have wondered all along if you were them. I know that you stayed with my Uncle JJ and Aunt Lynn and they never told us where you came from."

Huge smiles broke across Mo and Eli's faces as they nodded their heads up and down. The presence of God fell upon the men as they all started to laugh joyfully.

"You are the two witnesses that come in the last days, as the Bible foretells!" Pastor Terry exclaimed. They continued to smile and nod. Terry and Bobbi's mouths dropped open as they looked at each other. Even though they expected this to be true, they still felt a stunned emotion. They could feel the anointing of God on these men, and they knew it was true. However, they were so shocked that they had no words to say. Terry had a million questions coursing in his mind, but he held his tongue, waiting for a more opportune time. Right now there was a decision to be made and this was a decision that neither Terry or his wife Bobbi wanted any part of. They asked Eli and Mo to take sole responsibility of deciding their future. The two men had been prophesying and building up the believers in Jesus for a long time now and they had the respect and trust of everyone.

Claire Hollis, Ph.D.

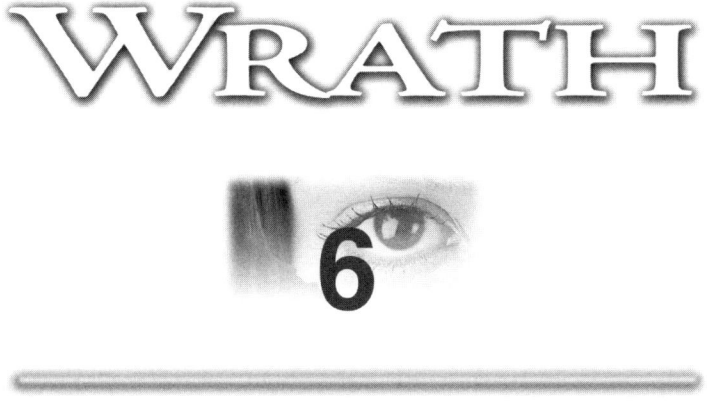

WRATH

Information was moving fast world wide. Computers were going constantly. Everyone was wanting to know what to do. Should we go to an airport or stay in hiding? Eli and Mo left Terry and Bobbi typing in information for all the anxious believers, and they went into the next room to pray and seek God's direction. They emerged with great big smiles on their faces. Eli spoke, "It's a trap, but God told us that you will be protected and not to worry. Tell everyone to go to the airport."

Eli looked at Mo and said, *"The time is right!"* Mo nodded his head and said, "Yes, it's time for Scripture to be fulfilled. The heavenly clock has been set into motion and we're part of the grand finale. I'm ready! This is the time I've been waiting for!"

There was an exodus of Christians from every continent. They had a communication system that could only have been made possible through the internet. Those who did not have a computer were in constant contact with those who did. They were coming out of caves, abandoned buildings, underground bunkers, boats on the water, and remote, uninhabited islands. They were clustered together in small groups. There was one thing that they all had in common. They loved Almighty God with all their hearts; they knew that Jesus Christ had come from God and had given Himself as the sacrifice for all the sins that they had committed. They knew that because of His sacrifice their sins were forgiven, and that one day they would live eternally in heaven. Their love for God meant more to them than their own life. They all felt that if God was willing to give His only Son Jesus so that they might have life everlasting, then the least they could do was to give up their lives for Him. They were all fully aware that King Catlin was the one that the Bible spoke of as being the antichrist. God had given all true believers supernatural knowledge about King Catlin .

Every believer was fully aware that they were living in the end times, and that very shortly it would all be over. Most were overwhelmed by the fact that they had been created and chosen and placed on planet earth for such a time as this.

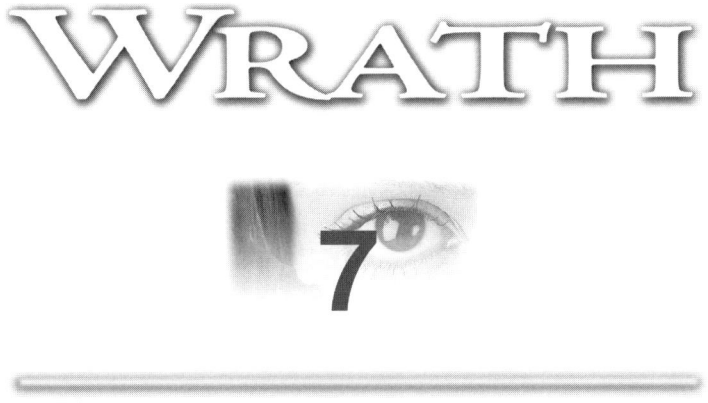

WRATH
7

Within one week every Christian believer was in the land of Israel. Their joy knew no end. People who were half starved were sitting down to hot meals. Being able to take a hot shower was like a gift right out of heaven. Most people came with only the clothes on their backs. They were all issued clothing from the worldwide government, enabling them to wash their personal belongings. The laundry rooms were packed with people singing and making merry. Many who needed medical attention were now being cared for.

The rest of the world was extremely confused by King Catlin's decision. They all loved and trusted him because he had brought peace. What about all these Christians? They didn't believe in *Unity* and they didn't bow down and worship King Catlin. What was going to happen next? These people could destroy all the good that Catlin had worked so hard for. Little did they know that Catlin's plans were to get them all out of hiding and in one place so that he could destroy them.

King Catlin challenged Eli and Mo to show up for a worldwide television debate the next morning at UTN. The meeting was set for 10:00 a.m., and all of the Christians were aware of it. They began to pray fervently, and their prayers were so powerful that the heavens opened up above the place where they were gathered and the glory of God descended down into the room where they met. All of the demonic forces on the earth began to get very nervous as they watched in the spiritual realm and noticed that as each Christian prayed, as the words came out of their mouths they flowed upward into the heavenlies. They hated the sweet smelling fragrance issuing forth as the prayers ascended up to God's throne.

King Catlin and Bishop John entered the UTN press room at exactly 10:00 a.m. These two had so much charisma and their appearance, with the long flowing robes and their crowns glowing like a laser show, was always breathtaking to everyone around. Eli and Mo were already seated and waiting for them. The room was filled with every kind of media personnel and full of tension and excitement at the same time. Reporters and cameramen were everywhere. As they walked into the room everyone (except Eli and Mo) bowed low before them as they headed toward their designated seats. There was quite a contrast in the seating arrangement. King Catlin and Bishop John were ushered to what looked like beautiful thrones and Eli and Mo were put into folding chairs. The television cameras immediately began to roll. If Catlin had known what was going to happen next he definitely would not have had it televised.

Eli and Mo rose from their seats and walked directly over to the two spectacular figures seated on their thrones, and Eli pointed his finger right into Catlin's face and declared," I know who you are. You better stop this masquerade or you'll be sorry." None of the media personnel understood that Eli wasn't speaking to the human named Catlin, but instead to the demonic power that possessed him. You could hear gasps across the room! Eli's gaze continued to pierce into King Catlin's eyes as Bishop John and Mo's eyes were also locked on each other.

King Catlin's face changed and it slowly became hideous. His eyes began to glow red with fire piercing into Eli eyes, he gets a mischievous grin on his face and began to snarl out of the corner of his mouth, "Remember that God created man lower than the angels. Well, you're human and we're not, therefore you can't touch us!" Eli staring intently at Catlin said, "We'll see about that! The Murphy family that you executed were very special to us."

With that comment Eli and Mo opened their mouths and fire proceeded like a blast from an opened door of a fiery furnace. Everyone was instantly consumed by the fire that came from their mouths. All the cameramen, the officials, everyone! No one was aware of what had just taken place, because everyone was burned by the fire with the exception of the unholy two. Everyone watching on TV saw the fire come from the mouths of Eli and Mo before they mysteriously lost their television reception. The most popular and famous newscaster, Tim Blake, missed all of the action as he was home sick in bed, watching this whole scene from his television set.

Bishop John and King Catlin quickly translated themselves out of the television studio and they were seen going into the temple in Jerusalem. They were unaware that this would be the last time they would ever have access to the restored Jewish temple. After spending some time there and soaking up the praises of the people, King Catlin meditated on what to do next. They translated themselves again and were seen entering the World Headquarters. Catlin immediately called a meeting of all their world leaders to be held the next day at noon.

Prophesied events were speeding up at a tremendous rate as the end time clock of God Almighty was winding down.

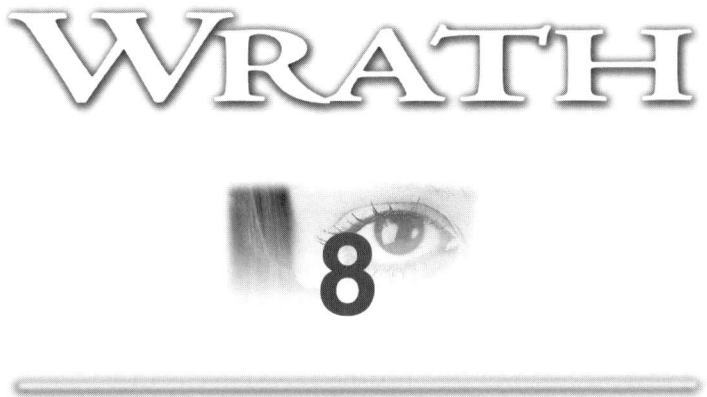

WRATH 8

Early the next day, leaders from all over the world began arriving at the World Headquarters. They all enjoyed the meetings because Catlin always had a fabulous meal prepared for them and let them enjoy it before he came on the scene. Because of the famine that they had all been experiencing in their lands they enjoyed these dinners because there were foods that were served to them that they had not been able to enjoy for a long time.

Just after the tables had been cleared, the King of the universe and Bishop John make their grand entrance into the room. Every man immediately bowed low to the floor with their face downward to pay them honor. How satan loved the worship! He could have stood there forever! He couldn't help himself! Lana had to nudge him to bring him back to reality.

Everyone was wondering what happened to Eli and Mo and what was taking place in Israel, but no one said a word. They all sat staring at Catlin stunned at the change in appearance that was slowly taking place before their eyes. His charming, handsome features had become distorted and the splendor of his garments seemed to fade. His crown was losing its glow.

King Catlin and Bishop John seated themselves on their thrones, and Catlin addressed the group. "Good day! I trust that you enjoyed the meal that I had prepared for your pleasure. Although there is a problem with the food shortage, at least we are experiencing peace. Everyone on earth belongs to the New World Order and the New World Religion. We are all one! We are all in Unity! That is, with the exception of these few Christian renegades that we have deceitfully rounded up and now have in one place in the land of Israel.

"I have called you all here so that you can have a part in deciding the fate of our enemies." Just as Catlin began to continue, suddenly the light in the room mysteriously disappeared! The sun had been shining through the windows of the room and now it was filled with a thick darkness. Puzzled, he fumbled over to the wall where he had seen the light switch earlier and turned on the lights. The stunned leaders jumped from their seats and ran over to peer out the windows to see what had happened. Why was it so dark outside in the middle of the day? All they could see were street lights beginning to come on automatically. Slowly lights started popping on everywhere. The darkness was incredibly thick. They turned to King Catlin with puzzled looks that demanded an explanation, but out of fear no one said a word.

Everyone thought that it was some kind of power outage, when suddenly the building they were in began to shake. At first the pulsating movement was light and then it began to increase until the large chandeliers above the table began to swing back and forth. Since King Catlin did not allow cell phones in any of his meetings, no one was able to call out in order to get information. There was a large screen TV in the corner of the room, and immediately Catlin ordered a little bald headed guy from China to run over and turn it on. To everyone's surprise a picture appeared. You could see the shock on the faces of all who were there, including Catlin himself, when they discovered that the problem wasn't a power outage.

The television channel was turned to Unity Television Network (UTN). There was Tim Blake. Although he had been sick and missed the recent debate, there he was on the television screen. He never looked like this before. In the past he always appeared cool and unemotional, but today he looked haggard and was in a state of panic as he said, "The sun has disappeared and the earth seems to be splitting at the seams! Major earthquakes are being reported from every continent at the same time! The entire earth is in total darkness and the temperature is beginning to drop, and it is beginning to get cold. Please, I appeal to everyone everywhere, conserve electricity until we find out what is going on. Our power plants will be overloaded so we need you to help out right now." Tim looking earnestly into the camera, "Sit tight and stay in your homes, don't panic, until further notice." The picture faded out and the screen went black.

All the leaders turned to one another in total panic. Mass confusion filled the room as everyone was speaking in their own languages. Everyone looked to their leader for help. King Catlin knew exactly what he was going to do. He looked at Lana, who stood frozen in Bishop John's body, and dismissed themselves to go into the next room to have a private discussion. He practically pushed Bishop John through the door and when they were out of view of the others, he slammed the door behind them. Catlin grabbed Lana by the hand, "Come on, we're getting out of here, we're going to confront those two in Israel. I'll have their heads for this and we'll wipe out those Christians at the same time!"

Within seconds they were standing in the room where Eli, Mo, Terry and Bobby were having a comfortable candlelight dinner. King Catlin kicked over a small table and pointed his finger at Mo screaming, "You're a dead man! You know who I am, and now I know who you are! We've met before thousands of years ago in Egypt." Catlin turned his head toward Eli, his face became twisted and his eyes began to glow as he sneered at him, " and I know who you are too! I didn't recognize you at first, but now I do. Remember Mt. Carmel? And how I was able to scare you away with my spirits of control that I had placed a mere human woman named Jezebel?"

Catlin continued, "I've got news for you! You think God's prophecies are all going to happen just the way He tells you they are, but it's all a lie! He doesn't want you to know the truth! *I* am the one that is in control. *I* will rule the world . *I* am going to get the other two- thirds of the angels on my side." Catlin straightened his shoulders and stiffened his neck as he declared, " Moses and Elijah, you don't have a ghost of a chance! You're following the wrong leader! If you will fall in with me and my team, I will give you my position and make you King of the universe!"

The four of them sat very calmly as they continued eating their dinner. The threat of Satan, and the loss of the sun's light didn't seem to phase them at all. They just ignored all of their remarks as they did the two of them standing there.

Satan had held his composure as long as he could. Now the real monster began to appear right there in front of them. He screamed at them, "BRING THE SUN BACK! I know you had something to do with this!"

They all looked up from the table and Eli said, "You can't touch me and you know it." Pastor Terry didn't even stand up, he just looked up and said, "In the name of Jesus I command you to go." Like a puff of smoke, Satan and Lana disappeared. Eli was smiling as the turned and looked at Terry. Terry shrugged his shoulders and said, "My uncle JJ taught me that!"

King Catlin was furious. He needed to be worshiped. That was the only thing that would calm his troubled spirit. He demanded that Lana get back to World Headquarters and give the leaders some new orders. He told her to have another statue of himself erected and he wanted all the world to bow to him in worship. He ordered fiercely, " Do it now! And make sure that it is shown on television every hour on the hour. The power plants are going to give out soon."

Mass confusion covered the dark earth as it continued to get colder. Thousands upon thousands had died in the earthquakes. The demons were going wild with excitement. To them this was a holiday. The more confusion, destruction and death, the more they enjoyed it. After all, their mission on earth was to kill, steal, and destroy, and they were having a party of all parties!

Claire Hollis, Ph.D.

WRATH

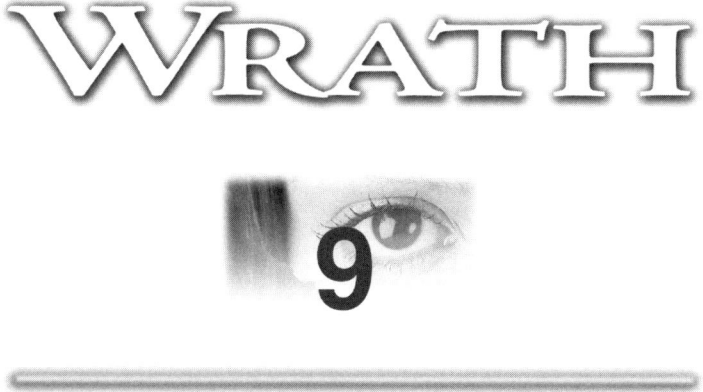

9

Pastor Terry and his wife Bobbi were praying together with their son Josh, when Eli and Mo walked into the room. Several days had passed since King Catlin had come into their dining room. The sun had resumed shining. Eli looked at them very lovingly and said, "Things are really going to get bad around here very shortly. Catlin is consumed with hate and has planned to kill everyone that has been brought to this place."

Bobbi's eyes immediately focused on her son Josh. She had so much love for him and she was feeling heartache as she studied him intently. The two of them looked more like brother and sister than mother and son. Both were blessed with the most gorgeous red hair. Bobbi's hair was dark auburn and cascaded softly down past her shoulders.

Both had beautiful deep blue eyes to compliment the red hair. Josh's hair was lighter and more of a strawberry blond.

Josh had matured a lot over the past several years. He changed from popular high school basketball player into a most incredible handsome young man. He was bright, full of wisdom and had a deep love for God. He was a man of few words, but when he did speak, it was with great wisdom mingled with a bit of humor which made everyone want to be around him. He stood taller than most, with his six foot five stature and broad shoulders. He was quite a striking individual. Bobbi on the other hand was cute and petite and looked much younger than her years.

Bobbi knew that God was in control of the situation, but she couldn't help but be concerned for Josh. It was only natural she was his mother, and she loved him very much. She then glanced at Terry, her dear husband. He looked deeply into her eyes and squeezed her hand. Bobbi could see a look of determination, along with peace in his eyes. Bobbi knew that her husband's deep faith came from being firmly grounded in the Word of God, and she smiled back. Peace fell over Bobbi as she squeezed his hand also.

Bobbi couldn't help but gaze lovingly at her precious husband. He was a very handsome man. Pastor Terry looked almost exactly like his father who had been killed along with his mother in an auto accident years earlier. Tall and very tailored, yet sensitive and caring. He was the type of pastor who had that special ability to be a mediator. Counseling was his speciality. He was able to calm the storm in any situation, and everyone absolutely admired and adored him.

He had committed his life fully to God when his uncle JJ had come to visit when he lived in Centerville, U.S.A. Uncle JJ had greatly influenced the entire family, and they all made decisions to follow Jesus to death, if need be. Now, it appeared that these decisions were becoming a reality.

Bobbi's thoughts were interrupted as Eli continued, "Satan himself has entered into the body of King Catlin. He has totally possessed it as you well know. The time of peace is over. Satan has been exposed and there will now be many wars and famines that will cover the earth. Many will be killed by hunger and wild beasts."

Suddenly, there was a knock at the door. Everyone looked at each other and Josh responded by moving quickly to open it, and you could see the excitement in his smile as he took his girlfriend Susie by the hand. After everyone welcomed her with warm greetings, Josh led her over to the sofa where they sat down comfortably across from Eli and Mo.

Eli continued, "I want every Christian here in Israel to eat the splendid meal that our enemies have prepared tonight . Tell them to have their traveling things ready to make an exodus after dinner. You will travel by night. God has revealed to me that He has a place prepared for every one of you. You will be safe there and absolutely no one is to leave from there once you arrive. At this place of safety, food and shelter will be provided and you are not to be afraid. God is going to reveal His mighty power. Eli glanced at Mo and they smiled at each other knowingly. "I guess you could say that God is going to *show off* tonight!" They all exchanged glances and chuckled softly in excitement.

"We won't be seeing you again until we meet in God's presence." No one expected that comment! They all embraced Eli and Mo and exchanged warm hugs. Everyone had grown to love these two, and just the thought of not being with them gave everyone a sad feeling, but the feeling was also mixed with excitement and anticipation of the great things God was about to do.

"Your spiritual eyes will be opened and you will be able to see the protecting angels that have been with you all along. They will show you the way. Hurry now and get your things together, eat your meal, and prepare to leave. Go quickly now and let the others know. YOU ARE A CHOSEN GENERATION, BORN FOR SUCH A TIME AS THIS. *Go Now!*"

Josh turned and looked deeply into Susie's eyes, he embraced her very tenderly. They had grown to love each other very deeply over the years. The kind of love that was a mixture of friendship, trust and admiration. With tears of love streaming down their faces they all realized that Eli and Mo had disappeared from their sight. Terry, Bobbi, Josh and Susie realized that time was short and they all ran quickly from the room to inform the others.

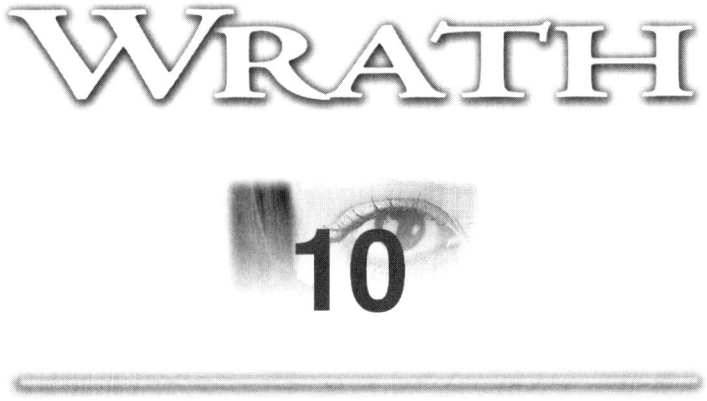

WRATH

10

The Catlin government was providing for the "renegades" with great grandeur. They were being provided with the best of everything. They were lodging in magnificent facilities and dining in the finest display of elegance. The Christians were unaware that Catlin's plan was to kill them the next morning. They were only told to prepare to leave. They were all relocated to the land of Israel. Even though the circumstances were foreboding, most were elated just to be able to set foot on the land where Jesus walked.

The instructions of Eli traveled fast among the group who had refused the computer chip identification mark, even though they were people of all nations and languages, everyone had been alerted. Because they were all united in one accord, communication was not a problem. Their hearts were knitted together with a common bond. They believed that the Bible is the true and inspired word of God, and that Jesus Christ is God's only Son. They believed that Jesus was sent to the earth to die for the sins of men so all could be set free from satan's bondages and be healed from their diseases by the power of God. They all had the assurance of spending eternity with Christ.

The Catlin military group called them for dinner at exactly six o'clock. Because of the volume of people, dinner was prepared and served in various designated dining rooms. It was very well organized just like everything else in Catlin's kingdom. At precisely seven o'clock everyone was escorted back to their quarters. News traveled like wildfire within the Christian camp and Susie, Josh, Terry, and Bobbi had been able to alert at least one person in every dining hall. By the time dinner was completed, everyone knew about the plan! Their excitement was beyond measure.

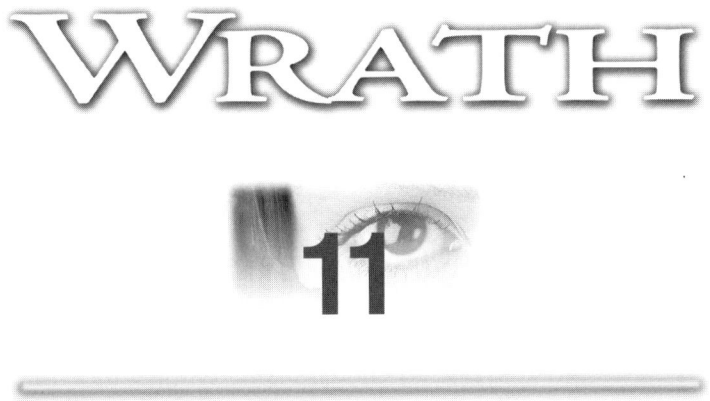

WRATH 11

Meanwhile back at International World Headquarters another meeting was about to begin. King Catlin and Bishop John were sitting on their elegant thrones placed at the head of the table waiting for everyone to arrive. Normally, the two would make a grand entrance after everyone had been seated in their designated places, but not today! The delegates were very shocked to see the two already in the room waiting for them.

This group of world leaders was only a puppet group. They were all like puppets dangling from a string and Catlin controlled the strings. The meetings were usually just a formality because they really didn't have any decision-making power. Catlin only used them for manpower that he needed from time to time. The only reason he had established the One World Order was for unity. He wanted these men to feel like they were important representatives.

World Headquarters was the most beautifully constructed building on the earth. It was the most spectacular sight known to man. It sat on a hill and had gates painted with gold. The winding street leading up from the gate to the building was covered with gold paint that shimmered brightly. Even the lamp post were covered with gold paint. When the sun's rays hit the building the gold sparkle of it could be seen for miles. It was truly a splendid sight to behold. A wrought iron fence painted with gold flaked paint surrounded the property to hold back the many spectators who would gather on the streets below every day just to get a closer glimpse of this magnificent wonder.

Everyone was now in their assigned seats and there was tension in the air, as they all waited in silence. When King Catlin stood to his feet, everyone automatically knew the meeting had begun. After slowly looking over all the men and giving everyone a sharp piercing look, he motioned with his hands for them to stand and then to sit back down. They quickly obeyed. He did this for no other reason than the power surge that it gave him. He loved the power that he had over men.

Everyone was aware of the changes that were taking place in the appearance of their leaders. The stones in Catlin's crown no long sparkled and Bishop John's beautiful white robe looked dull and dingy. Their faces were no longer handsome. Instead they looked more like monsters.

Catlin held up his right arm in their direction, "Leaders of the New World Order, I want you all to be aware of the plan that we have for these "rebels" who have chosen not to become a part of our united world system. They have come out of hiding from every country". He continued with a devilish smile, "We have reason to believe that every last one of them has left their hiding places and come forward." Catlin chuckled slightly to himself as he continued, " One thing about this group is that they are definitely in one accord and fervently follow the decisions of their leaders!"

"You remember JJ and Lynn Murphy? The two rebels we did away with for not accepting the computer chip? Before I killed them, they had two men living in their house and they immediately disappeared and we have been unable to apprehend them. These two men have become the leaders of this renegade group, and their every command is obeyed. These two are loved and highly respected by their followers.

Since we have a record of the entire world population in the Catlin Computer Bank, we know that we do indeed have them all, except these two men. The good news is that I believe these renegades have decided to trust us! Especially considering the fine treatment that they are receiving in Israel." Catlin glanced at Bishop John as he nodded back in agreement. The two snickered wickedly at each other.

He began to wave his outstretched hand, "What you all witnessed on TV recently was just a stunt performed by those two. That's why we immediately had the network cut off. We didn't want anyone to be deceived by the cheap little show that they were putting on!" Catlin knew he was lying, but then again, he was the father of lies. He couldn't help smiling smugly to himself.

"Here's the good news. Tomorrow morning we will be

rid of this stinking group once and for all. We have been treating them like royalty and they are living under a false security. In the morning when they come for breakfast, they will have a great surprise! The doors will be shut and locked behind them. Poisonous gas will be released into the air of all the dining halls and in seconds this planet will be clean and pure. Only the believers in 'Unity' will remain! Ha ha!" Catlin threw his head back and laughed triumphantly. "This is *my* earth, and it will be a paradise!" King Catlin sounded confident, although deep in his heart, he only hoped that he was right.

The men began to chuckle softly among themselves. They continued to snicker until it developed into an uncontrollable laughter. The laughter escalated into a loud roar which was heard all the way down the hill to the street where the spectators mingled.

WRATH 12

Satan had always believed that he was right and God was wrong and that someday he would be able to prove that the Bible was a lie. He envisioned the end quite differently from what the Bible predicted. He lived for the day that he could kick God off of his throne and take His place. Through the ages, he had contemplated how to establish his own throne and to achieve God's power. He dreamed of the day that he would become greater than God Almighty.

God in his fury, had kicked satan out of heaven like a flash of lightening. Down through the ages, the hate and revenge had festered in him like an open wound. *PAY BACK* was all he could think about, and to get even with God for what He had done to him was driving him constantly. It was always in his thoughts and plans.

Knowing that he couldn't get to God, he was doing the next best thing. He was attacking those who love God and consider Him to be their Father. He thought he had performed the ultimate revenge when he killed the Murphy family, but instead he just lengthened the time they would be with their Father eternally.

The memories of being kicked out of heaven became more vivid to him as he stood before the group of world leaders. An evil snarl appeared on his face and memories flashed through his mind. He stood there in a frozen position and was very quiet as he began to recall the past. The memories were so vivid it was as if it all happened yesterday.

He had been in control of the planet after he was able to deceive those first two humans that were formed by God. "Adam and Eve," God called them. Down through the ages there had not been much opposition to his program until Jesus Christ appeared on the scene. Satan (Catlin) prided himself on being the greatest deceiver of all. He was a master at it. Humans were so easily deceived. The most difficult task was to deceive the angels that knew Almighty God and had lived in His presence. It had been a challenge, but he had done it! He had succeeded in deceiving one third of God's angels who were kicked out of heaven with him. Now he ruled over all those angels and the humans on the earth, with the exception of the followers of Jesus Christ. The Christians had always been a thorn in his side.

King Catlin's eyes glazed over as he suddenly became absorbed in thought. He began to remember vividly that one monumental day in history as though it had just happened. He and his kingdom had killed Jesus Christ and they all witnessed his grave sealed and secured with armed soldiers. Next, the entire kingdom of darkness rushed to satan's headquarters for the greatest celebration party of all times. They all became very drunk with excitement and the feeling of victory.

Suddenly, the laughter and jeering ceased as Jesus Christ himself walked right through the door of the chambers where they were all having the party, very much alive and well! Jesus walked over to where he was sitting at the head of his long black table, and He stretched out His right nail-scared hand with His palm up and simply said, "Keys Please!" Satan reached down under the table and grudgingly handed Jesus the keys to death and hell. He was totally embarrassed, but had no choice but to obey. Jesus took the keys and very calmly turned and walked away passing through the door as if it wasn't even there. All the demons were overcome with fear, and they were falling all over each other as they cowered away from Jesus as He passed by them. Jesus knew every demon present and they all knew Him. After all, He was the one who had created them, and they all lived together before they decided to rebel against Him and He kicked them all out of heaven. This was the most humiliating day of satan's life.

Satan's fury knew no bounds! "Now this is the last straw! First the humiliation of being kicked out of heaven and now this, Jesus Christ had made him a laughing stock in front of all his demons. Although no one laughed out loud for fear of him. He knew that he had lost their respect. So now he had to indulge in the respect and worship that he was getting from the humans as he was walking around in King Catlin's body.

Claire Hollis, Ph.D.

WRATH

13

Catlin suddenly snapped back to the present and proclaimed, "We are one! World unity has now been achieved! Under *my* authority, we have achieved peace. Now I want you all to go back to your countries and proclaim to your people that I am to be honored and respected as the most holy one. Make it a law for everyone to pray and give thanks to me every hour. Make sure my emblem #666 appears on everything and I mean everything. That includes newspapers, television, all forms of media. I mean EVERYTHING!"

As he spoke his appearance continued to change. King Catlin wasn't even aware of the hideous metamorphosis that was taking place. He snarled, "Anyone who doesn't respond to my commands will be killed!"

The men exchanged fearful glances. They all had questions, but everyone was too afraid to ask. Finally one of the world leaders asked to be recognized. He was indeed a brave man full of courage. After being acknowledged, he stood to his feet and began to address Catlin, "What about those two weird looking characters that you were interviewing on TV? Before the program was cut off, it looked as though one of them created some kind of fire. It's been rumored that everyone and everything was consumed by that fire." The man shifted uneasily from one foot to the other as he continued, "I know you said that it was a stunt they were performing, but everyone is asking for an explanation." The man hesitated before saying, "People are beginning to think that *you* are the imposter, and not them. Everyone is very concerned and we want to know what to tell them."

At that remark, quick gasps were heard throughout the room, and then complete silence. Every man sat frozen, awaiting King Catlin's response. King Catlin lost all control now that he was being challenged. He no longer looked like the person they all had so deeply admired. Although he was still arrayed in splendor, his facial features were displaying his true colors. He began to look grotesque and his voice was growling.

He glared at the brave delegate standing in front of him. Pure hatred was penetrating from his eyes. He pointed his finger at him and immediately the man disappeared! The entire room was charged with fear. Catlin bellowed out, "Those two men are actors. You are not to pay any attention to them. I have given orders that they are to be killed on sight!" He slammed his fist on the table, causing the other men to jump in their seats. Catlin began screaming , "No more questions! Get back to your countries and keep peace and unity! You're dismissed!"

As the leaders scurried rapidly out of the building, they were talking in whispers between themselves. There was division among them. Some of them remained totally loyal to King Catlin, while others were quite disgusted with him. Much distrust was beginning to develop among the leaders.

Catlin heard Bishop John mumbling under his breath. Catlin screamed out, "What were you saying?" Lana had always been satan's next in command. She had been using the body of a petite woman before Satan had allowed her to enter the body of Bishop John. She knew everything that had ever happened on planet earth because she had always been with him. Normally she would have bowed down to him, but since she had been in Bishop John's body and he was in King Catlin's she felt like she was more his equal than his servant.

She stared directly at him, and without any fear she replied, "I know who those two are and so do you. You told us all that you were going to win in the end and that you would overthrow God. You told us that the Scriptures in God's word to man would never come to pass. Obviously the prophecy about the two witnesses is coming true right now. Now you tell me, how much more of God's word is going to happen?" Lana wanted answers!

Satan glared back at her. He grinned as he said, "The only option you have Lana is to follow me and believe that I'm right! When you chose to follow me you gave up all rights of ever going back. You belong to me now and that's a fact!" He lifted his chin and continued, "You have to choose me Lana, but I don't have to choose you. I've been stuck with you too long now, I'm sick of you! Get out of my sight, I never want to see you again!" Catlin didn't wait around to see what happened next, he simply vanished from the room.

Claire Hollis, Ph.D.

WRATH

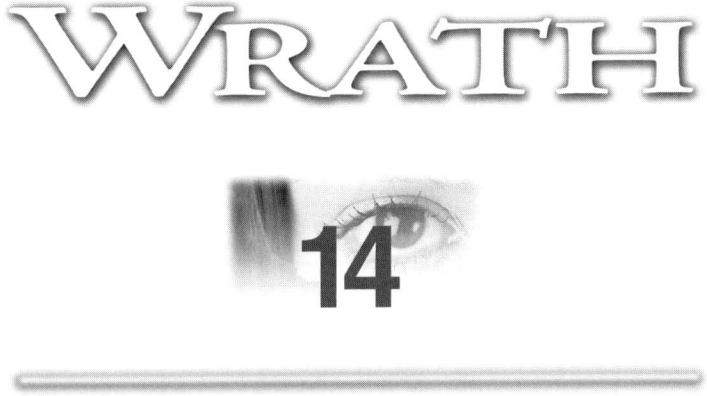

14

Now the inhabitants of the earth hated Eli and Mo. Their prophecies of mass destruction had made everyone uncomfortable. This had been going on a long time and everyone wanted to rid themselves of the *terrible two*, but no one could touch them because if they tried, Eli and Mo had the supernatural power to devour them with fire. These two had power over the waters to turn them to blood. They had the ability to strike the earth with plagues as often as they liked. And that was exactly what they were doing. The peace that the Unity Church had brought was now completely at the mercy of these two men.

That evening most of the leaders were still in their suites near the Catlin headquarters known as the King's Palace. They were making preparations to leave for their own countries, and most of them had their televisions tuned to UTN. Tim Blake, the most loved and respected newscaster came on the screen with the latest breaking news. He was interviewing the two men who had been the Murphy's houseguests and also Catlin was in the studio with them. Since UTN was owned by the Catlin empire, the broadcast was being aired live throughout the world.

Tim began the interview by commenting about their unattractive attire, which both men graciously ignored. Eli interrupted Tim's sarcastic remarks by saying," I bring very bad news to you inhabitants of the earth. Beginning immediately you can expect to see disaster strike the vegetation, the waters, and the heavenly bodies. You will see demonic locusts torment men for five months and then you will see a vast army of two hundred million appear and you will witness one third of mankind die." Eli leaned forward and looked directly into the camera, "Listen to me inhabitants of earth! Repent of your sins! You can avoid all of these calamities that are about to come upon you, if only you will believe in the Lord Jesus Christ and receive Him as the Savior of your life. I am speaking to any of you who have not taken Catlin's mark upon you. It's not too late if you will act now upon what I am saying !" King Catlin sat there with his mouth hanging open and the two men simply disappeared from everyone's sight.

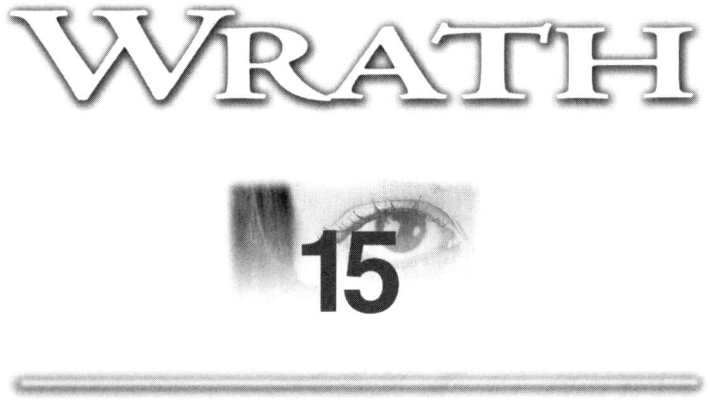

WRATH

15

Meanwhile, back in Israel, all the believers of the Lord Jesus Christ had been escorted back to their assigned areas. It was remarkable how quickly the dining halls had cleared. The word had spread that they would be leaving and everyone was excited. It was a miracle how the area had been evacuated and prepared for them. The miracle was the *true unity* of everyone involved. Thousands upon thousands had moved swiftly to make it happen.

As soon as they returned to their rooms, they began to prepare for their departure. Many of the guards who were assigned to each building fell asleep. The Christians were very orderly and formed a line and left the buildings very quietly and very quickly. No one knew where they were going, but everyone had faith that God would show them. It was a tremendous exodus! All of Catlin's forces were either blinded from seeing them or they were in a deep sleep.

Although there were guards posted at every entrance around the property, the Christians were able to pass right by them without being seen. Everyone exchanged smiles as they exited through the gates. More smiles came as they passed through every checkpoint unseen.

The Murphy family led the way. Pastor Terry, his wife Bobbi, their son Josh, along with his girlfriend Susie. Everyone was prepared to go anywhere and do anything that God wanted them to do. The word had spread like wildfire at dinner and everyone was expecting to leave that night. They had eaten a full meal and took only what they were wearing.

They were surely invisible, they weren't even detected on the surveillance cameras. Everyone was so amazed that they could walk right past the military personnel and almost touch them without being seen. This greatly encouraged their faith. The path they took was full of light even though it was dark outside. They traveled over mountains and into the desert. No one could see the lighted path except those traveling on it. They were all rejoicing with singing, clapping and dancing all the way. Mysteriously enough, no one could hear them either. No one minded the steep inclines or the narrow passageways. All fear was gone, because they knew God was in control and they trusted Him.

Josh and Susie were holding hands, as he led her down the path with the others. They both knew that they were meant for each other since the fifth grade. Except for a short period of time during their Senior year in high school they had never broken that arrangement. There was a few months that Josh was deceived by a young girl named Lisa, who had been planted in his home town for the very assignment of taking him away from Susie. Lana, who had been inhabiting the body of Bishop John had sent Lisa to their high school to destroy Josh and she had planned to destroy Pastor and Bobbi as well. Lana's plan was thwarted, Lisa was exposed and Josh and Susie were back together again. It was only a temporary break up of their relationship and since that time they have become even closer than before. Now they were both in their twenties and more in love than ever. They were so right for each other. They both loved God and their first priority in life was serving Him.

The Christian caravan has now been walking for about eight hours. Pastor Terry was very much in tune with God and heard His voice very clearly telling him they should all stop and rest for a couple of hours. The first eight hours of walking wasn't even tiring because of all the excitement, but now they were beginning to slow down.

Josh squeezed Susie's hand as they sat down to rest. He turned looking into her deep blue eyes. She looked so cute with her pony tail bouncing around her shoulders. He loved the cute little freckles that ran across her nose. She had a smile that could grab anyone's heart.

"Susie, I love you! " Josh stated passionately. We've been talking about marriage for years. The marriage application is still in effect. You know the one that we applied for before all of these things started happening in our lives. What's wrong with right now? My Dad could marry us! Please say you'll do it!" He looked pleadingly at her.

"Are you kidding?" Susie responded with a smile. "I have been dreaming of being Mrs. Joshua Murphy since fifth grade! I've always known that someday *the time would be right*, and I can't think of a better time than now. Yes! Yes! Let's go ask your father.

Hand in hand they approached Pastor Terry and Bobbi. Josh smiled as he said, "Dad, Mom, Susie and I want to get married!." Terry responded, "Josh, you aren't telling us anything new. We've always known that."

Josh laughed. He was so excited he could hardly speak, "No Dad, you don't understand! I mean, we want to get married now! Right here, right now! Right here in the desert!"

Terry looked at Bobbi and then turned to Susie. Susie's face was beaming so brilliantly that he knew that Susie wanted to be married right then also. Terry then looked back at Bobbi and smiled. No one could mistake the look of approval in their eyes.

"Praise The Lord" could be heard all over the countryside as it came bellowing out of the mouth of their leader, Pastor Terry. Word traveled like wildfire among the group as Terry and Bobbi were embracing Josh and Susie.

Susie's parents had been arrested and killed while they were visiting other family members in a nearby state several months earlier. Therefore, they just needed the approval from Josh's Mom and Dad. Almost everyone in the group had lost loved ones to the Catlin administration and the World Wide 'Unity' church.

The Christian community had always acknowledged the Murphy family as their leaders, so it was very appropriate for Pastor Terry to perform the ceremony. It wasn't anything that the Murphy's had done to acquire this fame; it was the plan of God. JJ and Lynn Murphy were deeply respected, and when King Catlin killed them, everyone immediately turned to their nephew Pastor Terry and his family for leadership.

Singing began and spread to the outer edges of the group, which was well over a mile away. Terry had performed so many marriages that he didn't need his format. Terry hushed the group and the wedding began right there in the sand.

The ceremony was so beautiful and everyone was so thrilled. When it came time to present a ring, Pastor Terry and Bobbi looked at each other in agreement. They had always seemed to know what the other was thinking. Almost in unison they said, "We want you to have these!" They both pulled their wedding bands from their fingers and offered them to Josh and Susie. Tears streamed down their face as they reached out their hands in acceptance of the rings.

"We also want to pass on to you the love, joy, happiness and peace that is reflected and symbolized in these rings." Terry continued. "May your life, no matter how long or how short be as ours is and has been. We have put God first in our lives and we attribute our success to that. Now we pray that you two will do the same. When God is at the center of a marriage and also of your lives, then all you can expect is something wonderful." Terry smiled at both of them, "No matter how tough times get or what obstacles come your way, it doesn't matter. You are never alone, because you are one with each other and one with God."

Pastor continued his blessing on them, "Like your Mom and I, we pray that you will think alike and know the needs of the other even without it being spoken. May the love that we have shared together now be passed on to you. God Bless You!" To climax the ceremony Josh and Susie exchanged rings with each other that they had just received from his Mom and Dad. When Josh kissed Susie, people were crying, rejoicing, hugging, and praying. Everyone's spirits were lifted by the wedding ceremony because they all loved the Murphy family so much.

Pastor Terry stood up on a high rock and announced that everyone was to take a couple of hours of rest before they continued on. There were plenty of caves in the area and crevasses in the rocks for the people to sit and lie down. A protective cloud appeared and hovered over them causing a cool refreshing breeze, and also hiding them from anyone who might be searching for them.

After the wedding Bobbi became overwhelmed with fear and bewilderment. That is, until she looked deeply into Terry's eyes and she was suddenly filled with security. She knew that her husband heard from God and that ultimately it was God leading and directing them to be in this place.

Mo and Eli were there to witness the wedding, although they were undetected by the Christians. Eli winked at Mo and said, "This is a picture of what will soon come to pass when Jesus Christ comes for His Bride." He glanced at the sea of people before him and waved his hand toward the group of believers. "There will be a great celebration and a feast at the marriage supper of the Lamb. The Lamb's wedding will soon come to pass, but for now the time has come to fulfill our part of these final days on planet earth." They nodded at each other, and walked off into the night.

WRATH

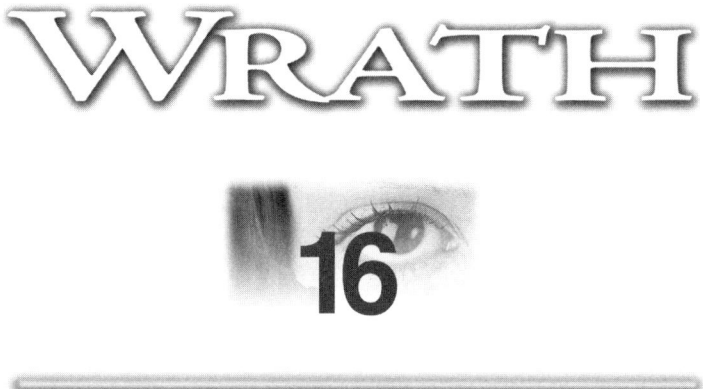

Moses and Elijah were seen on the Via Dolorosa in Jerusalem. Immediately King Catlin was informed. They were too close to Catlin's place of worship! They were on the King's territory and Catlin was irritated with that. This was his one place of refuge. He absolutely loved the statue that had been erected of himself, and the worship of the people that he received there.

Tim Blake and the UTN media crew were immediately on the scene. Sharp shooters were quickly placed everywhere in the vicinity of the two men, and the World Unity Military were on alert and arriving as swiftly as the wind blows.

The whole world was really quite intimidated by Mo and Eli. No one really wanted to come against them for fear of being burned to death. Everyone hated them because they kept prophesying doom.

Fear of their fire didn't phase King Catlin in the least. He really didn't care! Since he was a spirit he couldn't die anyway. Men's lives meant nothing to him, so he gave the command by cell phone to destroy the two, no matter what.

Elijah looked at Moses and said, "*The time is right! Our testimony is finished, or should I say, it is just about ready to begin?*" They smiled at each other as they walked down the street. There was the sound of much blasting and within seconds they were lying dead in the street of Jerusalem called Via Dolorosa. The World Unity Military had completed their orders. There was great rejoicing in the streets of Jerusalem as the people declared, "Now the world will be perfect!"

Tim Blake could be heard in the background instructing the camera crews to remain fixed on the dead bodies of the two men crumpled in the street. No one approached them and they were left lying there for all the world to see. Every media source was broadcasting the event live to the entire planet. People received great satisfaction from viewing the dead bodies on television.

A celebration broke out worldwide, and all of the inhabitants of the earth began to have a big party. This had been going on for three and a half days, as the men lay dead in the street. The earth's celebration had been continuous. They exchanged gifts, and chanted to one another, "No more torment! No more torment! Our enemies are dead!"

Tim Blake, who had witnessed this dramatic scene, had left only long enough to shower and shave. Then, he raced back to the old city to the location where the two bodies were lying. Tim wanted to be sure that he got the prime coverage and best pictures when King Catlin decided what he wanted done with the bodies.

As his eyes were fixed on the two dead enemies of the World Federation, Tim saw what looked like breathing, as their lungs suddenly began to expand and retract. He briefly glanced at his cameramen to make sure the scene was still being recorded. He wanted to be the first to broadcast this unbelievable sight. Tim's mouth flew open in shock as he witnessed the eyes of the dead men open. Moses and Elijah, who were laying in the street, turned to each other and exchanged glances as they winked and smiled. Then, to everyone's horror and surprise, they raised themselves up to a sitting position and then stood up and looked around. Screams were heard as the two men rose and began to dust themselves off.

The celebration that the people of the world had been enjoying for the past three and a half days was abruptly halted. A huge gasp could be heard from the people who were surrounding them and dancing in the streets. People were frozen in their positions staring at the two men who had been dead. Even the dogs stopped their barking and howling as if they also knew what was taking place.

Immediately everything became very quiet . Everyone standing around and everyone listening by way of media heard a thundering voice from heaven saying, *"Come Up Here!"*

Moses and Elijah slowly ascended up into the heavens. Just as the whole world had seen them lying dead in the streets, now everyone was witnessing them disappear into a cloud. All the nations of the world had their eyes fixed on the disappearing cloud. Tim Blake was in his glory, and none of this world wide observance could have taken place without the aid of the media.

Fear flooded those who were watching; those in person, those watching by television, and those who were observing the scene via their internet monitor. The television stations were repeating the scene over and over again until Catlin demanded them to cease. Catlin had already lost enough credibility and this current event was doing him the most damage of all.

In the same hour of the ascension of Moses and Elijah, the ground began to shake. People began to run and scream as a huge earthquake began to rumble across the earth. It was shaking everyone and everything as it split through the earth. Panic spread throughout the world!

Tim Blake was seen running through the streets, along with his camera crew, looking for a place of safety. His cell phone rang, but it seemed more like it was screaming at him. He jerked the phone out of his pocket as he was trying to hold on to a lamp post for safety.

"Hello? Hello?" Tim could barely hear his wife's voice on the other end. "Vicki, is that you?"

"Yes, it's me," Vicki's voice yelled back through the phone. "I'm OK!"

"Honey, I'm glad you're OK, but I can't talk right now. This is a reporter's paradise. Just watch the TV. I'm getting everything here live."

"Did you see those two that were dead come to life again?" Tim stopped running for a brief moment to talk.

"Now I'm beginning to wonder about all the Bible prophecies. We thought the Bible was a joke and we laughed at all that stuff, but now I'm beginning to wonder. I don't know when I'll be home, but I'm all right. Just watch TV."

Vicki hung up the phone and glanced at the television. Utter destruction and dead bodies were everywhere. She was so frightened that she curled up in the corner of the room and began to cry. The world was coming apart at the seams and all she could think about was her sister and all of the things that she used to tell her concerning the world coming to an end. Her sister believed in the Bible and kept telling her that she should accept Jesus Christ as her personal Savior, but Vicki thought it was all a big joke. She had been in complete agreement when Tim went to the Catlin authorities and turned her sister over to them as a part of the renegade group that everyone was searching for. She thought then that she was doing a good thing, but now she wished that she had her sister's Bible. That was impossible since Catlin had them all destroyed.

Claire Hollis, Ph.D.

WRATH

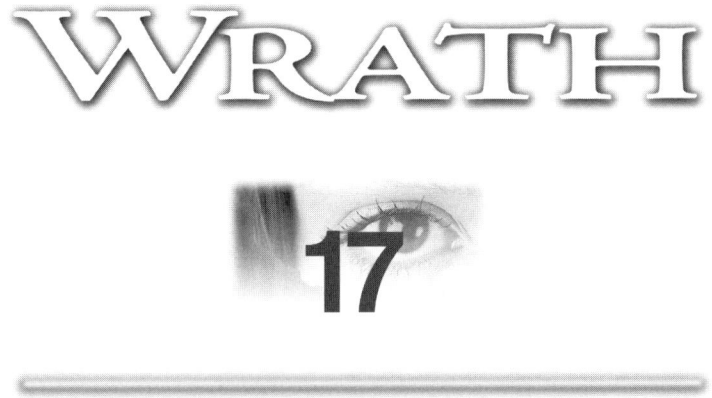

In Heaven there was great excitement and a tremendous celebration party. Voices were heard saying in one accord, *"The Kingdoms of the world are now the Kingdom of Christ and He will reign forever and ever."* What a scene to behold! Around the throne of God were twenty four elders. They all fell on their faces worshiping God and saying, *"We give You thanks, O Lord God Almighty, The one Who is and Who was and Who is to come. Because You have taken Your great power and reigned. The nations were angry, and Your wrath has come, And the time of the dead, that they should be judged, And that You should reward Your servants the prophets and the saints, and those who fear Your name, small and great, And should destroy those who destroy the earth."*

Claire Hollis, Ph.D.

WRATH 18

The renegade group, the ones that were chosen by God and the ones that had chosen God to lead them instead of King Catlin, were continuing their journey across the wilderness. Catlin was determined to find and kill them! His fury knew no end! When the Christians were discovered missing, he immediately gathered together every guard who had been on duty the night of their escape. He wasn't content to order their execution. He received much pleasure in doing it himself.

He knew the Christians were traveling on foot and he estimated that they were somewhere within a fifty mile radius of the location they had left. He surmised they must have taken the main road leading out of town to the south and into the desert. It was the road closest to the confined area where he had placed them.

He flew off in a fit of rage. He didn't go by plane or helicopter. He went by satanic means and translated himself all around the fifty mile radius and concentrated especially on the path that he thought they took. He couldn't see anything! They were nowhere in sight. God Almighty had shielded them from Catlin's view. God hid them just like He did from the guards as they left the city.

Satan had power, he was the ruler of this world, and God Almighty had not taken it from him as yet. King Catlin used that power and immediately ordered the Jordan River and the Dead Sea to flood the area where he thought the Christians might be.

Pastor Terry and his wife Bobbi, Josh and his new bride Susie were rejoicing along with all of the other Christians. They were singing and dancing along the path, knowing that they had been supernaturally protected.

Suddenly they heard a rush of water coming from behind them. Everyone stopped and turned in fear to see the rushing flood waters. People were standing speechless when Pastor Terry jumped up on a mound of sand and said, "Do not fear! Look ahead of you! *Don't focus on the problem. Instead, focus on the solution* that God has prepared for us!" Even though the group was large in number, it was a miracle because everyone was able to hear the words that Pastor spoke and in their own language.

The waves of the flood waters were gushing toward them and the sound was almost deafening. Suddenly, the earth opened up and swallowed the flood of water that was rushing toward them. Everyone watched in amazement as it happened.

When they turned back around to continue their journey, they stood frozen in their steps. They were in awe of the breathtaking scene up ahead. It was a paradise prepared for them. Beautiful huge gates stood in front of them with two angels posted on each side. The angels were adorned in garments of white. It was a bluish-white hue that no one had ever seen before. This beautiful light surrounded both of them. Each held a flaming sword and held it up over the big gates that they were protecting.

The angels smiled at Pastor Terry and one of them extended his hand and waved it toward the gate and bowed as he said warmly, "Welcome Pastor, please bring your people and come and rest. You will find comfort and peace here." Then both angels opened the wide gates as God's people began to enter.

Supernatural peace flooded their souls as they entered through the gates. It was such a powerful experience as their spiritual and physical strength increased. The beauty of this place was beyond description. Rivers of water so clear that you could see the bottom, beautiful plants and flowers, and luscious fruit hanging from the trees. The depth of the colors was so intense that people were rubbing their eyes in disbelief.

Josh squeezed Susie's hand so tightly that she just melted with emotion because of her love for him. She wasn't by herself anymore and she felt so secure just being next to him. Susie had always loved being next to Josh's tall athletic frame. She was so petite she always had a feeling of protection being with him, but now that they had entered the gate there was even more security that went far beyond that of earthly love. Josh slowly turned to her, "Susie, I think God arranged for us to have a honeymoon in paradise." Tears began to stream down Susie's face. The expression of love that flowed between their eyes was exactly what God had in mind when he created marriage.

Mike, Cindy, Tim and Matthew were the last four people of the Christian group to walk through the gate. Whenever the last person's foot touched the ground in the paradise area, the two angels shut the gate. The two glorious angels stood on each side of the gates and as they pointed their flaming swords toward each other. The entrance was sealed, and there was nothing that King Catlin could do about it.

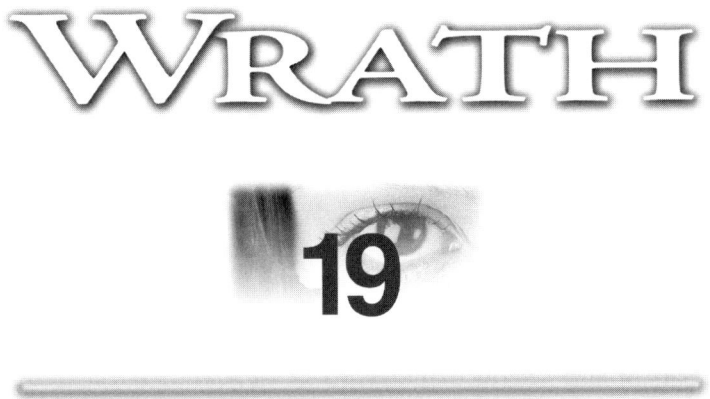

WRATH

19

King Catlin's demonic forces were getting nervous and discouraged. Lana was furious! She knew all too well that God was the victor of this battle. She had lost all confidence in the lies that satan had been telling her.

The battle through the ages has always been good versus evil. Lana thought to herself, "It's amazing how satan, (Lucifer, as he was called back then) could have convinced one third of us to follow him. He had deceived us into believing that evil would win out over good in the end He convinced us that he would be in control of everything, and that by following him we would become the *heirarchy* of the new kingdom." "Ha!" Lana sneered with disgust. "Satan is the greatest con-artist of all! He is the father of lies, and has been a deceiver from the beginning."

God's wrath was coming to planet earth and she knew now that she and the demonic kingdom could not escape it either. Satan was right, there was no turning back. She had made her choice!

For the first time since she had been hurled to the earth along with satan, Lana allowed herself to remember what heaven was like. She remembered the beauty, the peace and security, but most of all Lana remembered the love. She remembered how perfect things were until Lucifer decided that he was going to kick God off of His throne and take His place. Lana remembered the wonderful praise and worship and the beautiful feeling that came from worshiping God.

Her thoughts switched instantly from the warm feeling of God's love to a negative feeling when she thought of Lucifer who had been in charge of the music and all of the beautiful worship in heaven. He had been created with such splendor. Lucifer had been placed in one of the highest positions of authority in heaven. She remembered that he had one of the top three positions under God's leadership.

When he rebelled against God, his appearance changed. The ugliness that was on the inside of him altered his appearance on the outside, until he was hideous. Satan had the ability to deceive and to change his features at will, but Lana knew what he really looked like. She saw it happen again just recently when the handsome face of King Catlin slowly began to change into the grotesque figure that he really was.

God loved her so much. Lana had been in the highest position in the heavenly choir, and Lucifer was what the humans would have called the choir director. Lana sighed. It hurt to let herself remember. Satan told them that he could read their minds, therefore no one dared to think about it for fear of him. Now, Lana questioned even that. She mused under her breath, "I bet he really can't read our minds, it was probably a scare tactic to put fear into us in order to control us!"

She knew what the Bible predicted. She knew and understood it even better than the humans. After all, she was around when the Scriptures were being written. She knew that God's wrath was quickly approaching. She knew that not only were all of Catlin's followers in trouble, but she and the entire demonic kingdom were in trouble too!

Claire Hollis, Ph.D.

WRATH

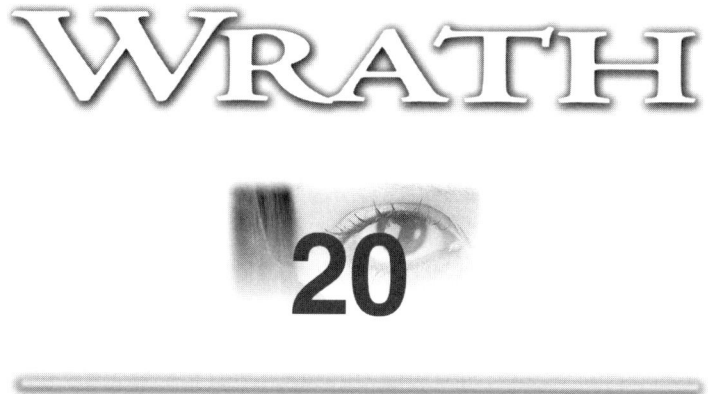

A few months had passed. The earth and everyone on it was in complete turmoil, with the exception of the Christians who were enjoying the paradise that God Almighty had prepared for them.

Conditions on the earth were horrible. It was extremely chaotic. The earth had gone from peace and unity to distrust and fear. Men were running in fear and panic, people were screaming and blaspheming God.

There was something significant about one third of everything on earth. No one could understand it. One third of all the vegetation and grass was gone. One third of the sea had become blood. One third of the sea creatures and ships were destroyed. One third of the sun, moon, and stars were struck. The day did not shine for one third part of it. Even one third of the inhabitants were killed by an army of two hundred million. Everyone was asking each other, "What is significant about one third and what does it mean?"

Men were dying from the bitter waters. No one could understand it. The wise scholars of every nation were searching for answers. One researcher came up with a Biblical explanation and when King Catlin heard of it he was furious, and in a fit of rage had him executed immediately.

Great swarms of locusts began to sting and torment the people who were left on the earth. They tried everything they could think of to get rid of the pests, but to no avail. The people wanted to die, they longed for death, but death wouldn't come. For months the people were tormented constantly. The sting that came from the tails of the locust caused the most horrible pain known to man. The whole earth was filled with screams coming from the victims who were being stung. Finally after five months of torment, the locusts mysteriously disappeared.

Tim Blake was discussing the woes that were being poured out on the earth with his wife Vicki, one night as they were preparing for bed. They agreed together that they did not see how things could possibly get worse. Life on earth was truly a living nightmare.

Tim woke up the next morning to a ghastly foul smell in the room. He turned toward Vicki and gasped in horror. His beautiful wife looked like a monster. He jumped from his bed and ran into the bathroom where he looked in the mirror at the loathsome sores that were on his face too! He ran back to the bedroom and frantically shook his wife. Vicki opened her eyes and began screaming in terror. They both began to tear at their faces, but the pain from the sores was too great.

Little did Tim Blake, and the rest of the people who had survived the past few months of destruction, realize that the wrath of God had come, and was being poured out from heaven and things were soon to get much worse.

Tim had always wondered if the Biblical explanation for the destruction occurring was true, but his broadcasting position had always prevented him from making a clear decision about Godly things. Several people had called him and expressed their thoughts about the Bible and the Bible predictions, but Tim had chosen to ignore their warnings. He was not one to go against King Catlin especially after he had executed the scholar.

Claire Hollis, Ph.D.

WRATH

21

Meanwhile, the people of God that were living in paradise surroundings were experiencing more love, joy, peace and happiness than they had ever known. Everywhere they looked was beautiful. The numerous colors of the garden were vibrant and radiant. The fruits and vegetables were so delicious and satisfying that the people of God could hardly believe it. It seemed like everything there was constantly worshiping God. One blade of grass would touch the other and it was as if they were in a praying position. The branches of the trees reached toward heaven in worship, and even the sound of the rivers and streams were singing praises to the Lord. Josh and Susie were truly having a honeymoon designed in heaven!

Pastor Terry and Bobbi were no longer needed to lead the people. They were completely surrounded by beauty and peace, and it was beyond the comprehension of human words or expression. The people of God praised their great Creator, and their souls were tremendously satisfied. It was a continual time of praise and worship.

Lana was allowed to observe all that was going on, although she could not enter into the area because of the angels with their flaming swords who were guarding the entrance. She was so jealous as she thought to herself, "These people of God are stealing what I used to have whenever I was in the Heavenly choir under Lucifer's direction." She remembered how it felt and knew exactly the joy they were experiencing. She was sick with grief as she watched them and murmured bitterly, "These humans have taken my place and there is nothing I can do about it."

Just as the Bible predicted, the earth's water turned to blood and every living sea creature died. Tim Blake was furious! Seafood was his favorite delicacy. Most of the restaurants had closed down when one third of the seas were struck. A few restaurants did remain open, catering to those willing to pay the extremely elevated prices. But, now with this new catastrophe, there would be no more lobster, no more shrimp, and no more fish! This was total, and it was worldwide!

People of every nation, race, and tongue had hardened their hearts. Now they were more determined than ever to survive whatever came their way. The Unity Church had brought them together, but all the calamities had bonded them like super glue and they were determined to fight. Most of them realized by now that it was God who was in control and they blamed Him for their afflictions. They were so full of revenge that they were determined to seek vengeance against God.

Tim Blake appeared on UTN and instructed the people to restrict the use of all the water, which included bottled water. It was to be used for drinking purposes only. Blake instructed everyone to collect rain water. At his instruction, every country on earth implemented systems to do so.

Everyone was determined to overcome the calamities. They were all so furious that they were resolved to overthrow whatever was causing the world destruction. Everyone was on a suicide mission. They were willing to sacrifice their lives if necessary to save the world.

Everyone looked to King Catlin for direction. They had no other choice, he was their only hope. Even the demonic kingdom, who knew that God's plan was being fulfilled as predicted, had to follow him. Most people had chosen to ignore the prophecies completely, even though God had warned in the Bible of the destruction. The humans were oblivious as to what was going on, but the demons knew all too well what to expect.

The death and destruction brought great delight to the kingdom of demons because of their great hatred for the human race. They were all experiencing the ultimate of satisfaction that a demon possibly could. Every day was a holiday! There was just one little damper on the situation and that was the fact that time was getting short and they all knew what their future held.

Just when men of the earth thought that they had the water problem solved, an intense heat covered the planet.

The days began to get hot—then hotter until the people of the earth struggled to endure the scorching heat. It was like walking through fire. In fact, many could even see the fire. Some were burned so badly they were unrecognizable. The enormity of the situation had caused all of the hospitals to overflow, along with the doctor's offices. It became each man for himself and there was almost no help available.

All the inhabitants of the earth decided that God was their enemy, and they hated Him all the more for what was happening to them. They were not looking to the Bible for answers, and they were not even trying to find out what was going to happen next. They blamed God for everything and continued to blaspheme Him daily.

Claire Hollis, Ph.D.

WRATH

23

World Headquarters managed to survive the wrath of God that was being poured out on the world, and continued to stand in all of it's splendor. King Catlin was seated on his throne inside this magnificent edifice. Since satan had chosen to enter into the body of King Catlin, he was not exempt from the suffering of the plagues that had come upon the earth. He resented the fact that he had to enter into a human body in order to accomplish his mission to take over the world. Satan was unable to accomplish this in his spiritual body, so he was forced to achieve his goal in human form. He had to enter a human in order to take over the world. He was not exempt from the sores that covered everyone's body. He hated God so much!

Throughout the ages, satan had been quite successful in his revenge on God by stealing, killing and destroying the human race that God had created. He knew that by hurting the humans, he was ultimately hurting God, and he found great pleasure in that. However, now satan was getting the blunt end of God's wrath by taking on this human form.

Tim Blake was busy covering a story on the disappearance of the Christians, which they always refereed to as the *rebellious renegades.* Suddenly, and without warning, Catlin and his world kingdom were plunged into total darkness and everyone was experiencing intense pain like never before. This included King Catlin!

No one could explain this mystery, but did the people repent? No! They just gnawed on their tongues from the pain and they continued to blaspheme God. The cursing was worldwide, and it was so loud that it could be heard throughout the universe.

Tim Blake immediately called his wife Vicki on his cell phone. She began to curse and scream like a wild woman. Tim's conversation with his wife was interrupted and immediately cut off when he heard Catlin's voice break in through the receiver. King Catlin was in pain and he was screaming orders at him. He was able to break into any of Tim's conversations in order to have constant communication with him.

Tim responded immediately. UTN was the only worldwide network operating, so he went before the viewers instructing them to conserve their electricity, and to use candles for light. Tim announced that everything was under control and this was only a temporary outage. He was trying to convince the public that this problem would be solved shortly and that they could all work together in *Unity* and overcome.

The people began to rise up with boldness, instead of shrinking back in fear. They were determined to fight this problem at all costs. King Catlin had brainwashed them into believing that their power came from within themselves and that they could accomplish anything if they would use that power from within. He wanted to teach people that they can do all things themselves and that they don't need anyone or anything else. This was a lie and one of his greatest ways of deceiving the human race. It was that same pride that got him kicked out of heaven and now he wanted to use the same thing to destroy the earth's people. No one that was left on the planet understood that all power comes from God Almighty, and they could not fight against God and win.

By this time Catlin had all the Bibles destroyed. If they could have looked into the Scriptures, they would have known what to expect next. But because this was not possible, they were oblivious to God's Word. They remained in spiritual darkness, just as the earth remained in physical darkness!

More unexplained events occurred. The great Euphrates River suddenly dried up. It was as if the River had never been there! The hole where the water had been was filled in with earth and became flat land. One could walk completely from one side to the other on dry land.

King Catlin now hated the city of Jerusalem, a place he once cherished. Before, it had brought him great pleasure because of the praise and worship that he had received there. He had desecrated the Jewish Temple and had received much pleasure in doing so. But now that pleasure had worn off.

He hated Israel because it had contained God's chosen people, and the entire area had become repulsive to him. He had tried on numerous occasions throughout history to destroy the Jewish population, but had failed every time.

It reminded him of the time, two thousand years ago when he had brought Jesus Christ up to the pinnacle of the temple and tried to convince Him to jump off and test God. He was trying to tempt Jesus and told Him that God would send His angels to save Him. Jesus didn't fall for his trick and satan was discouraged because his plan wouldn't work.

He was remembering how he had tempted Jesus and failed. The memory of how he thought he had destroyed Him in death, only to find Him alive a few days later always tormented him. He recalled the day Jesus walked boldly into his headquarters and demanded the keys of death and hell from him. He hated the humiliation of Jesus walking in and breaking up the biggest party of all time that he and his demons were having! They were all celebrating the victory of Jesus' death, and there he stood right in the middle of them, alive and well! The victory party was abruptly over, and he was left discredited.

This time Satan was determined to win. He thought to himself, "God thinks that His Bible prophecies are going to come to pass and I'm going to prove Him wrong! I will get rid of His Jewish people, *once and for all!*"

WRATH

24

King Catlin quickly contacted all the world leaders and convinced them to unite together against the nation of Israel to destroy it. He devised a plan that he thought would work. He decided to use the miracle of the Euphrates River drying up to his advantage. He said, "I will send my troops from the East moving across the dry ground for a surprise attack. Then we will attack Israel from all sides. I want ships stationed in the Mediterranean on high alert and ready to send smaller boats to shore with soldiers and artillery for a surprise attack."

This was an unnecessary move for Catlin, since he was already in control of the world and this included Israel, but his hatred for the people chosen by God had completely consumed him. Since he could not find the Christians who had disappeared, he had turned his revenge and anger toward Israel. Every memory associated with that nation created a stench in his nostrils.

Jesus Christ was born there, He had shed His blood there, and died for the sins of the world. Jesus had risen from the dead there, and He started His ministry and established His church there. The church had continued down through the ages and it was that same church that all those rebellious renegades were a part of!

Satan couldn't stand the memories; they were driving him crazy! He had to get rid of the people and every place that haunted him. He knew, all too well, every holy location in the land of Israel and just exactly what had taken place there. Either satan himself had been on location during the event, or his demons were assigned there and reported back to him everything that occurred.

After Jesus rose from the dead and ascended back into heaven, satan stayed in his headquarters most of the time running his kingdom from there, until the time that he decided to enter into the body of Catlin.

WRATH

25

The remnant group were suddenly removed from their hidden place of safety, and they found themselves moving through the air at a tremendous rate of speed. SWOOSH--in an unexplained second, they found themselves in the center of thousands of people. When each believer looked at each other they noticed that they were all dressed alike. Joy flooded each one as they noticed their surroundings.

A celebration was going on in the heavenly realm, and what a party it was! It was the party of all parties. It was the celebration that all Christian believers had been waiting for. It was called the Marriage Supper of the Lamb. Jesus Christ was the Bridegroom and the Bride consisted of those who believed in Him and obeyed His Word. The Murphy family had been reunited together again. It was a wedding feast that had been prepared by God Almighty Himself.

Everyone had their appointed seat, and Jesus Christ rose from the head of the table and began to serve the meal Himself. Can you imagine being served dinner by the King of Kings and the Lord of Lords? Each person that He approached He knew intimately. He knew everything about them, having been with them their entire life. They knew Him intimately also. They had put their faith and trust in Him over and over again throughout their years. Now they were reaping the rewards of that belief.

The Christians were all dressed in robes of white linen, and they were in new bodies that were incorruptible. They could never die! All of the pain and all of the sadness were gone. Everything that satan had brought upon them on the earth had disappeared, and God had replaced the darkness with His glorious light. This place was pure. There was peace, love, and truth. The evil that they had known on the earth was eliminated, and now they were in a heavenly paradise. The riches were so common that even the streets were made of pure gold.

After everyone had finished their meal, Jesus Christ stood up and said, "There is a final battle to be won!" Suddenly, there appeared a white horse standing at attention right behind the chair of each person at the banquet table. Without Christ giving them further instruction they knew immediately what to do. As they mounted their own private stallion, each horse turned toward Jesus Christ.

The appearance of Jesus suddenly changed from the humble Lord who had just served them dinner to that of a Mighty Warrior. His eyes were like flames of fire, and on His head were many crowns. His white robe had been dipped in blood, it was His own blood. It was the blood that Jesus had shed on the cross at Calvary, and God Almighty had held it in reserve for this very moment. Writing on his robe declared, KING OF KINGS AND LORD OF LORDS. Everyone saw a sharp sword coming out of His mouth. As He mounted His horse, the same words were seen written on His thigh, KING OF KINGS AND LORD OF LORDS.

A loud voice was heard by all. It was a mighty angel calling all of the birds together to inform them of the great feast they were about to have. The birds would devour the flesh of earthly kings, captains, mighty men and even the horses that they sat upon.

The heavens opened and all those dressed in white robes and the white horses could see King Catlin and all of the satanic kingdom, Lana and all the leaders of the earth gathered together to make war against the Jewish people. The horses of Jesus Christ and His bride were moving at a tremendous speed. When they reached the earth, King Catlin was the first to be captured with Lana being the second. King Catlin was heard shouting, "I told you I never wanted to see your face again, Lana!" But before he could speak again both of them were cast alive into a lake of fire burning with brimstone. Both antichrist and the false prophet would be together. Everyone else was killed with the sword that proceeded from Jesus Christ. The angel was right! All the birds were filled with the flesh of men and animals alike. This battle took place in the land of Israel in the Valley of Megiddo at a place called Armageddon.

A mighty angel appeared coming down from Heaven, having the key to the bottomless pit and a great chain in his hand. He laid hold of the dragon, that serpent of old, who is the Devil and Satan, (the one who gave power to the antichrist and false prophet) and bound him up and he cast him into the bottomless pit and shut him up, and put a seal on him, so that he should deceive the nations no more.

Old things had all passed away by now, and all things had become new. The ones whose names were written in God's Book of Life would experience eternity with Him and would rule and reign. No more death, no more pain, only the love and security of being with the One who created all things. The One who was willing to give up His life in order that they could experience life eternal with Him.

"It is done!"

Echoed from Heaven

God's Wrath was complete ....well, at least for a thousand years!

The Wrath of God is surely coming to planet earth. If you do not want to be a part of it and you have made the decision that you want to spend eternity with God Almighty, then repeat this prayer:

Heavenly Father, I truly believe that you sent your only son Jesus to come and to pay the penalty for my sin by dying upon the cross. I accept him as my personal Savior and ask you to forgive me of anything that I have ever done that displeases you in any way. I have broken your rules and have sinned and I am sorry. I want to live the rest of my life acceptable to you. Thank you for your grace and salvation. In Jesus name, amen.

Claire, and her husband Paul, minister internationally and have seen thousands of people freed from demonic influence. They each hold a degree of Ph.D. in Clinical Christian Psychology, and conduct private and group counseling sessions. They also conduct seminars and teach a School of Deliverance.

Other books from Warfare Plus Ministries

THIS MEANS WAR! - A complete guide to the teachings of Christ on deliverance, along with many other biblical references regarding deliverance. Sadly, deliverance has been treated almost like a forbidden topic in the church realm. THIS MEANS WAR! teaches in great depth everything you always wanted to know about demon warfare and the supernatural, but have been afraid to ask!

DEMON SLAYERS - Actual case histories of people who have gone through deliverance. Relive the experiences with them as this book takes you through shocking, extreme, intense battles of Good versus Evil—and Good always prevails!

THE LIGHT - Go on an adventure with JJ and Lynn as they visit a mysterious town. The curtain gets pulled back on some fascinating, supernatural things that have been covered over for years. JJ and Lynn get into trouble and find themselves in life-threatening situations.

Get to know Lana, who states, "I hate those two! Our leader hates them, too. And his number-one goal is to completely destroy them!"

DELAYED INVASION - A U.S. military crew in Germany mysteriously intercepts a plot by demon entities to overthrow the governments of the world by disguising themselves as beings from outer space. Go with JJ and Lynn as they visit Washington, D.C. and get caught up in the middle of the invasion plans.

DECEIVED- Unable to invade planet earth in *Delayed Invasion*, the demonic kingdom has developed a new master plan. Discover what that plan is, how the Heavenly forces combat it, and what JJ and Lynn do when they once again find themselves in the middle of a life-threatening spiritual war.

If these books are not yet available in your local bookstore, order them direct by e-mail, calling, or faxing our Tampa office.

Warfare Plus Ministries offers many tape series on special demonic warfare issues and mini-books on individual stronghold forces. For a listing of our ministry tapes, manuals and other materials, visit our web site or write to us. You may also request a product order form at the same address.

If you are interested in attending a group seminar or want to schedule a group seminar in your local church, please call or write to us.

Paul and Claire Hollis
Warfare Plus Ministries, Inc.
3457 W. Kenyon Avenue, Tampa, FL 33614 USA
Phone (813) 935-4673 • Fax (813) 935-2387
E-mail: WarfareP@aol.com • Website: www.warfareplus.com

Claire Hollis, Ph.D.

Description	Quantity	Unit Price	Total Cost
Books			
This Means War		$12.95	
Demon Slayers		$11.95	
The Light		$11.95	
Delayed Invasion		$11.95	
Decieved		$12.95	
Audio Cassettes			
Exposing & Expelling Strongholds (4 tapes)		$20.00	
Don't Get Caught In Satan's Web (2 tapes)		$10.00	
Are U Cursed? (2 tapes)		$10.00	
Power & Authority Over Evil (2 tapes)		$10.00	
If I'm Supposed To Be Gay... (2 tapes)		$10.00	
CD's / PowerPoint			
Exposing & Expelling Strongholds		$40.00	
Don't Get Caught In Satan's Web		$10.00	
Are U Cursed?		$10.00	
Power & Authority Over Evil		$10.00	
Exposing & Expelling Strongholds*		$60.00	
*NOTE: This is a data file CD with presentation slides and files, not an audio CD			
Videos			
Exposing & Expelling Strongholds (4 videos)		$80.00	
Deliverance From Satan's Torment		$20.00	
Workbooks			
Exposing & Expelling Strongholds		$20.00	
New Beginnings in Jesus Christ		$20.00	

Call for International shipping

		Subtotal
Payment ❏ Check	USA Shipping & Handling <10 .... $3.00 $10-$25 .... $5.00	
❏ VISA ❏ MasterCard ❏ Discover ❏ AMEX	$25-$50 .... $6.00 $50-$75 .... $8.00	Shipping
Credit Card No. _____ Expiration ___	$75-$100 ...... $10.00 $100-$500 ...... .8% Tot $500> .... .7% Tot Int'l Orders .... Call for $$	TOTAL

Please Print Clearly

Name: _____

Address: _____

City: _____

State: _____

Zip: _____

Send To:

Warfare Plus Ministries
3457 W. Kenyon Ave.
Tampa, FL 33614

Fax: (813) 935-2387
Email: WarfareP@aol.com
www.WarfarePlus.com